Distributed in the United States by NorthSouth Books, Inc., New York 10016.
Library of Congress Cataloging-in-Publication Data is available.
ISBN: 978-0-7358-4273-1 (trade edition)
1 3 5 7 9 • 10 8 6 4 2

Printed in Poland by Drukarnia Interak Sp. z o.o, Czarnków, October 2016

www.northsouth.com

SLOPPY

Wants a Hug

By Sean Julian

North
South

"*Can I have a hug,
please?*"
asked Sloppy.

"No,"
said Dewdrop.

"Why not?"

"You know why not."

"I don't know what you mean."

"Yes, you do," said Dewdrop. "You're just pretending not to."

Sloppy tried to get a hug by being sad.

*"And don't think crying will get you a hug.
I know you're only pretending."*

Sloppy tried to get a hug by giving Dewdrop presents....

"I don't want a stick ...

"...or a big rock."

"You know you're not supposed to pull up the flowers."

"I've told you before ...

"... woodland animals are not presents."

Dewdrop gave rabbit a big hug to
say sorry for Sloppy's behavior.

Which made Sloppy very jealous.

"I thought you weren't giving hugs today."

"Everyone can have a hug today,"
said Dewdrop.

"Everyone except you!"

This made Sloppy very sad, and this time he wasn't pretending.

"*I'll go away then.*"

Sloppy went and sulked under a tree.

Tweet!
(Help!)

Tweet!
(Help!)

"I didn't want a hug anyway."

"Can I help you, little birdie?"
                                asked Sloppy.

Tweet! Tweet!
(I fell from my nest.)

Tweet! Tweet!
(Thank you, Sloppy.)

Sloppy very carefully
lifted the little birdie
back into its nest.

Dewdrop saw how helpful
Sloppy had been.

Dewdrop said,
  *"That was a nice thing you did Sloppy.
  I think you deserve a big hug."*

"*Not sure I want one anymore,*" said Sloppy.

But of course he was only pretending.

Sloppy hugged Dewdrop,
and Dewdrop hugged Sloppy.

It was a lovely hug, and Dewdrop
almost forgot why she didn't want
a hug in the first place.

Until Sloppy did
what he did best . . .

He gave her a great big **sloppy**

lick.